D1384887

ISBN 0-448-40058-8

90000

9 780448 400587

1

SPINE CHILLERS

THE GHOST IN THE MIRROR
AND OTHER GHOST STORIES

BY JIM RAZZI

Cover illustration by Jacqueline Rogers
Illustrated by Karin Kretschmann

PUBLISHERS • Grosset & Dunlap • NEW YORK

Contents

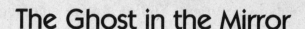

The Ghost in the Mirror

ANDY SAT AT the big bay window of the rented beach house. He watched a gray cloud slip past the white moon. Then the moon's reflection re-appeared on the dark sea.

"Perfect night for reading about ghosts," Andy said to himself. He took one last look out the window. Then he returned to his book.

Something he read made him grin. He turned to his nine-year-old sister, Lisa.

"How would you like to see a real ghost?" he said.

"What are you talking about?"

Andy showed her the cover of the book. The title was *How to Conjure Ghosts*.

"The easiest ghost to call up is a mirror ghost," Andy said. "You have to stand in front of a mirror. You repeat the name of the ghost you want to see. Then it appears in the mirror."

"Oh, sure," said Lisa. "The only ghost you'll see will be yourself. You're always standing in front of the mirror, combing your hair. I get tired of watching you."

"Ha, ha," said Andy. "Well, I'm going to try it, whether you like it or not."

"I don't like you to do weird things when Mom and Dad aren't home," Lisa said.

"They're only at the Brewsters' house, right down the road," Andy replied. "Look, I should be out at that amusement pier," Andy went on. "Instead I have to baby-sit for you. I think I deserve a little fun."

"What's fun about ghosts?"

"I'll call up one that's fun," Andy answered.

"Well, *you* can do what you want," Lisa said. "But I'm going up to the bedroom to watch TV." With that, she turned and climbed the creaky stairs.

Andy stood in front of an old mirror across from the bay window. The book said that he should stare into the mirror. Then he had to let his mind go blank. Finally he had to repeat over and over the name of the ghost he wanted to see.

Now that Andy was about to do it, he couldn't think of anyone to call up. It doesn't matter, he thought. Nothing's going to happen anyway.

So Andy just stared into the mirror and let his mind go blank. He chanted in a deep singsong voice, "Any ghost, any ghost, any ghost . . ." He let his eyes close. . . .

Andy opened his eyes slowly. Nothing. He knew it. Wait a minute. What was that? Andy thought he saw, reflected in the mirror, a shadowy shape by the bay window behind him.

No. It was gone. Probably nothing there to begin with.

Andy was just about to continue his chanting when he saw it again. This time there was no mistaking it. The figure started to become clearer. It was a man wearing a striped jersey and floppy pants cut off at the knees.

Andy spun around, but nobody was there. He turned back toward the mirror. There was the man again. Now Andy could even make out his face. It was dark and scowling. Over one eye, he wore a patch.

The man in the mirror began to move toward Andy. As he did, he drew out a sword—a pirate sword!

This can't be happening, Andy thought. I didn't really call up a ghost. But there wasn't any other way to explain it.

Andy spun around once more. He hoped he would see a real person. Anything but a ghost. But there was no one. Gathering all his courage, he faced the mirror again. The pirate was no more than ten feet away from him. Andy sniffed the air. The salty smell of the sea began to fill the room.

Now Andy could see that the ghostly figure was dripping wet. Pieces of seaweed hung from his legs. It must be a drowned pirate, called back from his watery grave. Called back by *him*!

As Andy stood there shaking, he suddenly heard the front door open. A voice called, "We're home, kids!"

Without looking into the mirror again, Andy

ran to the front door. His mother and father were standing there, smiling at him.

"How are you doing?" his father asked.

Andy wasn't about to tell his parents anything. He wasn't sure he believed it himself.

"Uh, great, Dad," he finally answered. "I was just going to watch some TV with Lisa."

Andy believed that as long as he didn't look into a mirror, the ghost had no power over him. So without another glance in the mirror, he went upstairs and joined Lisa. She was watching a comedy. Good—just what he needed.

Lisa looked up at Andy and asked, "So did you see any ghosts?"

"Don't be silly," he answered. "I was only kidding you."

But he couldn't keep his voice from trembling.

The next morning, when Andy woke up, he almost forgot what had happened the night before. Then he remembered. Funny how the mind can play tricks on a person, he thought. But all the same, he kept away from mirrors all day.

That night Andy, Lisa, and their parents went

into town. A small boardwalk ran along the beach. On a pier that stretched out from the boardwalk was a small amusement park.

To Andy the amusement park was the only reason to go to town. But his father and mother wanted to shop. So they made a deal. They would drop Andy and Lisa off at the pier. In an hour they would pick up the children.

Andy and Lisa waved good-bye to their parents and walked onto the pier. There was a ferris wheel, a small roller coaster, and a carousel. But Andy was drawn to the fun house. At the door stood a huge mechanical clown. It was holding its stomach with two hands and laughing like a maniac.

Andy couldn't decide whether or not to go in. He had had all the scaring he needed for a while. But then he saw two cute girls his own age buying tickets.

"Want to go in?" he asked Lisa.

"No," Lisa said. "I don't like fun houses. They're supposed to be fun, but all they do is scare me."

Out of the corner of his eye, Andy saw the two girls enter the fun house. "I'll go by myself," he said. "But stay right by the ticket booth, okay?"

Lisa promised that she would. Andy bought a ticket and hurried in, hoping to catch up with the girls.

Andy found himself in a dark hall. He could hardly see in front of him. He felt his way along the walls. Then suddenly he entered a dimly lit, oddly slanted room. He saw the two girls across the room. They were laughing as they tried to keep their balance on the tilted floor.

When they saw Andy, they whispered to each other. Andy gave them a friendly smile and tried to catch up with them. But they left the room with a giggle and a quick look back at him.

Andy followed them into another, larger room. He was looking so hard for the girls that he didn't notice what kind of room it was. Suddenly he sucked in his breath. He realized he was in a *mirror* maze.

Andy could hear the girls laughing somewhere

in the maze. But that wasn't enough to keep him going. He stumbled around, trying to get out the same way he had entered. But he couldn't find the way back. He would have to go through the whole maze.

"Take it easy. Nothing's going to happen," he told himself. "Just take your time. You'll get out the other end."

But at each turn Andy became more confused. He couldn't hear the girls anymore. He was alone in the maze.

With a sob of fear, he stumbled around a corner. He came face to face with himself in another mirror. But he was not alone. In the mirror, gliding toward him, was a small figure. He had no doubt about who it was—the pirate ghost!

Andy whirled around, only to find another mirror. There was the ghost again, getting closer. He ran around corner after corner. But each time he found still more mirrors. Wherever he looked, he saw the ghost. And each time, it got closer and closer.

Now Andy saw that the pirate had the sword clutched in his bony hand. Andy was paralyzed with fear. His legs felt as if they were stuck to the floor. He was certain that, as soon as the ghost got close enough, it would come out of the mirror after him.

His mind told him he must do something. The pirate was no more than a dozen feet away now. The wild cruel look in the pirate's eye was horrible. And his leering mouth, opened wide in triumph, was worse.

I could close my eyes! Andy thought suddenly. Maybe that would stop the ghost. But how can I ever get out of here with my eyes closed?

Maybe someone will come, he thought.

Andy couldn't wait for that. The ghost was almost to the edge of the mirror. So he quickly shut his eyes.

He stumbled against one mirror after another, trying to find his way out. For a second he opened his eyes. To his horror he saw there were mirrors in front and in back of him. The ghost was no more than a foot away!

9

Suddenly the arm with the sword came out of the mirror. It was just as if the mirror were a pool of water.

Andy expected the pirate to strike. But instead the pirate's eyes widened in surprise and anger. He was looking past Andy toward the other mirror. There, too, stood a scowling pirate with a sword. The ghost was looking at its own reflection.

Andy had a wild idea. Just as the pirate raised his sword, he threw himself to the floor. Quickly he crawled out of the way.

Andy felt a whoosh of air as a blade lashed out at the spot where he had just been. His idea had worked. The ghost in the mirror thought its reflection was an enemy pirate. The ghost had forgotten all about him. It was too busy fighting itself!

As Andy crawled farther out of the way, he saw the ghost raise its sword high. It aimed a mighty blow at its reflection, and the two mirrors cracked into pieces.

Sobbing with relief, but still scared, Andy

made himself examine the two smashed mirrors. There was no trace of a ghost.

When Andy reached the exit, he took a deep breath of fresh sea air. He walked shakily toward his sister and waved.

"Did you have fun in there?" Lisa asked.

"Not exactly," Andy replied with a weak grin.

"What happened?" asked Lisa curiously.

"You wouldn't want to know," Andy said. "Besides, you wouldn't believe me."

Lisa just stared at her brother.

Andy silently vowed never to look into another mirror as long as he lived. But then he looked down the pier and saw the two girls from the fun house.

Well, he thought, maybe just long enough to comb my hair. And he hurried his sister along the pier toward the girls.

The 13th Floor

JIMMY RYAN RAN down the street, dribbling an imaginary basketball. He stopped and faked a pass. Then he took a shot at an imaginary basket.

"Ryan scores again!" he said. He grinned at himself in a store window.

It was a school holiday. Jimmy's new friend, Peter Sanchez, had invited him over to spend the afternoon at his apartment. They were going to play video games.

Peter lived in a brand-new high rise. It looked at least forty stories tall. When Jimmy entered the lobby, the doorman asked whom he was visiting. The man called up to Peter's apartment, 29A.

After the doorman gave the OK signal, Jimmy

13

strolled over to the elevators. He pushed the UP button.

While he waited for an elevator, he pretended he was an astronaut. "Are you ready, Ryan?" he said under his breath.

"Roger, Mission Control," he answered his own question.

Just then, the elevator to his right opened. It was empty, so he stepped in and turned to face the door. "Mission Control," he said, "this is Ryan. Ready for blast-off."

Jimmy pushed the button for Peter's floor— twenty-nine. The elevator door swished closed. Suddenly Jimmy almost felt as if he *were* going up in a rocket. Before he knew it, he was at the tenth floor.

Pressing against one wall, he watched the small black screen over the door. Red numbers winked on and off: 11, 12 . . .

At 13, the elevator whooshed to a stop. Jimmy guessed someone was getting on. But when the door opened, no one was there.

Jimmy peeked out. No one was down the hall either. He stepped back into the elevator and waited. The door stayed open. He jabbed the button for the twenty-ninth floor again. But the door didn't close.

"I guess it's stuck," he said to himself. "I'll just have to walk up."

He tried the button one more time. When nothing happened, he sighed and stepped into the hall. Jimmy noticed that the gray tile floor was worn and dirty. The overhead lights were dusty, old white globes. And the walls needed a good coat of paint.

Boy, they must have run out of money when they got to this floor, Jimmy thought. He shrugged and looked for some stairs. But there was no sign of any.

All he found was another, shorter hall. He saw that it led to a third hall that ran the same way as the first. Together the three halls made an *H*.

A strong smell suddenly filled Jimmy's nostrils. Jimmy stopped, sniffed, and looked around. Thick black smoke was pouring into the hall. It was a fire! Jimmy had to get out of there and call the fire department!

Gagging and coughing, he ran down the short

hall to the other side of the building. The smoke followed him. He could hardly see.

Jimmy saw a red exit sign at the far end of the hall to his left. He ran for the door. He grabbed the knob and turned it. It came off in his hand.

He sucked in his breath. He knew he shouldn't go into an elevator during a fire. But now he had no other choice.

With his heart pounding, Jimmy raced back to the elevator. Trembling, he reached for the lobby button and pushed it. But the elevator didn't move. Just then he heard screams coming from down the hall.

He stuck his head out of the door. Two kids bolted from the short hall. They raced down the elevator hall away from him.

"Hey, you're going the wrong way!" he yelled.

Jimmy was torn. He wanted to go after them. But a blast of hot, smoky air sent him reeling backward into the elevator. In a panic, Jimmy started to push all the buttons.

"Come on! Come on!" he screamed.

He was still yelling when the elevator door suddenly closed.

Jimmy slumped to the floor, coughing. Suddenly he felt the elevator move. He couldn't tell if it was going up or down. When the elevator stopped, he looked up. He was on the twenty-ninth floor.

With a rush of relief, he scrambled out of the elevator and into the hall. He ran past a row of doors, looking for Peter's apartment. But even in his haste, he noticed something strange. This hall had plush blue carpet. It had clean white walls and modern lights. Even the shape of the floor was different. There was one long hall and a shorter one at each end.

Jimmy finally found Peter's apartment at the end of one of the short halls. He pounded on the door.

A few seconds later, Peter opened the door. When he saw Jimmy, he cried out, "What's the matter with you? You look like you've seen a ghost."

"There's a fire on the thirteenth floor. Quick! Call the fire department!"

Peter looked at Jimmy strangely. "You're out

of breath," he said. "You didn't run up twenty-nine floors, did you? Have a seat and rest."

"Rest?" Jimmy repeated as he fell into Peter's apartment. "There's a fire on the thirteenth floor!"

"Take it easy," Peter said. "Is this some kind of joke? There *is* no thirteenth floor in this building."

"W-what?" Jimmy looked puzzled. "But I just came from there!"

In a rush of words he told Peter what had happened.

As he finished, Peter's mother entered the room. Jimmy repeated his story. He saw her glance toward her son. "You think I'm making this up, don't you?" Jimmy asked. "Or that I'm crazy or something."

"No, of course not," Mrs. Sanchez said. She didn't sound very sure. "But there isn't a thirteenth floor in the building," she continued. "And certainly no floor looks like the one you described.

"Many people think thirteen is an unlucky

19

number," she went on. "So in some buildings the floors go from twelve to fourteen.

"Besides," she continued, "at the first sign of smoke or heat, our fire alarm goes off in the whole building. It's been as quiet as a tomb all morning."

Jimmy shook his head. He couldn't have imagined the whole thing. But he could see it was no use trying to convince Peter and his mother of that. So he just accepted their offer to wash up and have some orange juice.

When Peter's mother left the room, Peter looked at Jimmy earnestly.

"Look," he said, "there's a handyman in the building named Harry. He's lived in the neighborhood for years."

"So? What's that got to do with anything?" Jimmy asked.

Peter shrugged. He leaned toward Jimmy.

"All I know is that Harry thinks the building is haunted."

Jimmy sat up straighter. "Can we go see him?" he asked.

Peter nodded.

*　　*　　*

Harry, who looked to be at least sixty-five, was in the basement near the boiler room. Jimmy repeated his story for Harry. The handyman scratched his chin and got a faraway look in his eyes. Then he said, "You know, another building used to stand on this very spot. It had a thirteenth floor. There was a terrible fire fifteen, twenty years ago. Quite a few people were hurt. In fact, I think that a brother and sister were killed. They lived on the thirteenth floor."

A chill came over Jimmy, and he felt goose bumps go up his arms. Then he had a wild thought.

"Do you think I saw the ghosts of those kids?" he asked.

"Well, now," Harry said. "I've never told anyone this before. But once in a while, when the elevator passes between the twelfth and fourteenth floors, I think I hear children screaming. But I say to myself that it's just the wind in the elevator shaft."

Then Harry looked at the two of them.

"Doesn't do for old Harry to talk of ghosts," he

said. "Someone might think I wasn't quite right in the head and couldn't do my job."

He winked at them. "I have to get to work," he said. "I can't stand around gabbing all day." Then he shuffled off.

As Harry left, Jimmy felt Peter nudge him.

"Aw, let's just forget the whole thing and go out. I think Harry's probably kidding us anyway."

"What . . ." Jimmy looked puzzled. "Oh, sure, okay."

They spent the afternoon in the park. By dinner time Jimmy was feeling better.

Peter said, "Hey, there's a great monster movie on TV tonight. Want to come over after dinner and watch it? You could sleep over."

When Jimmy thought about riding the elevator again, he felt scared. But he didn't want Peter to think he was a baby. So he said, "That's a great idea. I'm sure my mom will let me."

"Great! See you later, then," said Peter.

After dinner, Jimmy stood in front of Peter's building. He still felt no less scared. Finally he got up his courage and walked in.

There was a different doorman. Jimmy told him where he was going. Seconds later Jimmy was standing in front of the elevators. This time both of them were there with the doors open.

He tried to get his feet to take him into one of them. But they wouldn't move.

"Something wrong, kid?" said the doorman.

Jimmy was miserable. What could he say?

Then Jimmy made up his mind. He lifted his feet and marched into an elevator. He pressed the button for the twenty-ninth floor. He held his breath.

The elevator rose. Jimmy looked at the numbers as they went by, his heart thumping with each one.

10, 11, 12 . . .

I'm going to make it! he thought.

Suddenly the elevator lurched to a stop. The door opened. He was on the thirteenth floor again! This time Jimmy didn't wait to start pounding buttons. But again nothing happened.

It was then that Jimmy smelled smoke. His body felt cold and his legs trembled. The whole thing was happening again. That made him think of the kids. He might have saved them if that blast of hot air hadn't sent him back into the elevator.

He raced out of the elevator and headed straight for the other side of the building. He stopped near the exit door. Smoke was starting to spread through the hall. He didn't even know which apartment the kids were in.

Then suddenly a door opened. Seconds later he saw the same two kids rush down the hall.

"Come on, Willy!" said the girl. Her voice sounded strange.

Jimmy was so amazed that at first he couldn't speak. Then the girl tripped and the boy almost fell over her. Jimmy finally found his voice.

"This way!" he yelled. "There's an exit here."

The girl got up and grabbed the boy's hand. They dashed down the hall toward Jimmy. The smoke was getting thicker, but Jimmy held the door open as the children ran up to it. The girl was about his own age. The boy looked so much like her that he had to be her brother.

The kids scrambled through the exit. Jimmy

was about to follow them. But a blast of hot air ripped the door out of his hand. It slammed shut. He grabbed for the knob. To his horror, it came off, just as it had before.

The smoke was so thick that he could hardly see. He knew his only hope was to get back to the elevator. He raced down the hall, gasping and coughing. He rounded one corner, then another. The elevator was still there—just like the first time!

Jimmy tumbled into it, falling to the floor. He was too weary even to get up and hit the button. All he could do was lie there, panting and coughing.

Suddenly, the door swooshed closed by itself, and the elevator started to move. Jimmy dragged himself to his feet. His chest was heaving up and down.

Then, as if nothing had happened, the elevator stopped on the twenty-ninth floor. The door slid open.

Jimmy staggered out and pulled himself together. He didn't want to repeat what had happened that morning.

When Peter opened the door, he looked oddly at Jimmy, the way he had earlier in the day.

But Jimmy only said, "Hi."

"Well," said Peter, "are you ready for two hours of horror?"

Jimmy went blank. Then he realized Peter meant the monster movie on TV. "Sure," he said.

Later on, during a commercial, Jimmy said to Peter, "I was thinking about something. Harry did say that those two kids were killed in the fire, didn't he?"

"What?" Peter answered. "Oh, that. No. As a matter of fact, I was talking to him just before you came up. He was here fixing our faucet. He just left. Harry said he remembered now that the kids were saved. They claimed that some boy they had never seen before came along. He led them to the fire stairs. They never figured out who that kid was."

Jimmy was startled. "Are you sure?"

"Yes," said Peter, punching him on the arm. "Now, how about if we just watch the show?"

Shark!

THE HUGE JAWS of the shark were no more than two feet away. But Tony didn't blink an eye. The jaws were *all* that was left of the shark. And they were hanging on the wall of his grandfather's living room.

It was summer vacation. Tony had never been to his grandfather's house before. He had made the trip across the country all by himself.

Tony's grandfather, Paul Rivera, had been a fisherman all his life. Now he didn't fish anymore, except for fun. He had filled his small house on the beach with all kinds of things from the sea. But the sharp-toothed shark jaws were his prize.

Tony's grandfather came into the living room and smiled. Earlier he had looked his grandson

27

over closely. He had said proudly to Tony, "You look just like I did when I was young."

Now he said, "You like my collection? Maybe you will make your living from the sea, too."

Tony nodded. "Did you catch this shark, Grandpa?" he asked.

"Ah, the great white shark," Mr. Rivera said. He scratched his beard and smiled again. "Not all by myself. I had some help.

"It was a day much like this one. I was a young man. For two months a great white shark had been seen near the shore. Everyone became afraid to go into the water. We had a town meeting. We decided what to do. A few other young fishermen and I would go out to kill the shark.

"We had only spear guns to fight the shark. I can't tell you how many times we speared that fish. Finally it died. We pulled it to shore.

"It was then that we got a good look at it. The shark's big head was full of scars. Many of them were old scars. I guess other men had tried to kill it, too.

"Also, the shark had only one eye left. As it lay on the shore, I'm sure I saw that eye look right at me. It was as if the dead shark was trying to remember my face so it could somehow get even.

"All the same, I cut out the jaw. I took it home with me—and there it is." He pointed proudly to the wall.

Tony had listened to the tale with wide eyes. As his grandfather finished, the old man patted him on the head and smiled.

Mr. Rivera paused, then continued. "In spite of everything, I felt a little sorry for the shark. After all, it was only doing what came naturally. It had the bad luck to come in contact with men.

"You know," he went on, "there is one more thing. For the last fifty years from time to time people claim they have seen the shark. They can tell because of its one eye and the scars. Some people think its ghost haunts these waters."

Tony's grandfather shrugged. "Of course, that's just an old sea tale. I for one have never laid eyes on another shark around here since that day. Ghost or not."

A few days later, Tony went out on the water in a small boat. He and some older boys were going diving together. "Stick close to your buddy," said John, the boy in charge. Tony had listened. But at one point, a sudden big wave carried him away from his buddy. Tony wasn't worried. The boat wasn't far away, and he was a strong swimmer.

All at once the water became strangely still. It turned as cold as ice. Tony looked toward the boat. Two boys were still on board. But it seemed to have stopped bobbing up and down in the water. The boat looked as if it was in a photograph.

Tony had a sudden urge to get out of the water as fast as he could. He tried to swim for the boat. But his arms felt as if they were made of lead. He could barely move them.

Then suddenly the water lifted Tony up several feet. Something was making huge waves. Tony turned his head around quickly.

Not more than ten yards away was the shape of a giant white shark. It was heading through the waves right toward him!

Tony tried to swim again, but he just splashed weakly. He swallowed some sea water and

gagged. For all his effort, he got no closer to the boat.

What was the matter with the boys on board? Tony thought. Couldn't they see that he was in danger? Couldn't they row toward him?

Tony tried to yell. But his voice wouldn't rise above a whisper. He looked behind him again. There was the shark with its head just above the water.

It was a great white shark. It had scars all over its head. One of its eyes was missing. His grandfather's shark! It had to be. But if so, it must only be a ghost. *Only a ghost!*

Closer and closer the shark came. When it was almost on top of him, it opened its huge mouth. Tony stared in surprise. Even in his panic, he noticed something strange. The shark had no teeth!

At that second the shark crashed into him. Tony thought he would be pushed under the water or caught in the shark's toothless mouth. But he felt nothing at all. It was as if the shark had gone right through him. It was as if Tony were no more solid than the water around him.

Tony watched in amazement as the shark's fin

sped away. Then it disappeared. At that very second the boys in the boat seemed to come alive again.

So did Tony's arms. He found he could swim. He cut quickly through the water and dragged himself up onto the boat.

"Did you see it?" Tony said, out of breath.

"See what?" the boys answered.

"The shark," Tony replied.

The boys shrugged and looked at each other. One of them—Steve—said, "What's with you? You were staring at that water. But you didn't move. We almost called out to see if you were all right."

Tony just looked at Steve and didn't say a word.

Back at the house, Tony told his grandfather what had happened. The old man nodded.

"So the tales were true," he said. Then he paused and his eyes widened. "I'll bet that ghost thought you were me. It came back for revenge."

Tony looked up at the jaws hanging on the

living room wall. An idea flashed into his mind.

"No, I don't think it wanted revenge," he said. "It can't hurt anybody now. I think it just wanted its teeth back."

Tony looked at his grandfather pleadingly. "Could we throw the jaws back into the sea?" he said. "If we do, maybe the ghost shark won't return."

His grandfather looked at him in surprise and scratched his beard. "Maybe you're right," he said. "Maybe even a shark has the right to rest in peace after its life is over."

The next morning Mr. Rivera and Tony went out on the water. Tony helped his grandfather lift the shark jaws and toss them gently into the calm sea.

Ghost Writing

I WAS SITTING at my desk, wishing I were somewhere else. My teacher, Ms. Hanover, was flipping through some papers. I knew what was coming—a test in American history. Last year I had enough trouble remembering what happened in my own state. I'm sure I can't remember what happened in the whole country!

Soon I would be getting another *F*. Ms. Hanover had given me a lecture about my grades just the other day.

"You're not stupid, Janice," she had said. "In fact, I think you're quite bright. Your problem is that you're lazy."

I'm not lazy. I just like to daydream. Mostly I daydream about what I'll do when I grow up. I'm going to be a famous writer and autograph my best-selling ghost stories.

I really believe in ghosts. Once on TV I saw a seance. That's where you sit around a table and hold hands and call for a spirit to talk to you.

Anyway, I was wishing someone else could take the history test for me. That way I could spend the time thinking up ghost stories.

Under my breath I said, "If anyone out there wants to help me, feel free to do so."

Suddenly a pencil lying on my desk began to move. I did a double take, like in the cartoons Was I seeing things?

The pencil stood up at an angle, as if someone were holding it. Then it started to write on a piece of paper in front of me. It wrote, "Hello, my name is Flora."

My mouth dropped open. I just stared. No one seemed to have noticed the pencil. And I didn't want to tell anyone about it. I was sure I was going crazy.

After the pencil finished writing, it just fell over and lay still. I picked it up. It was freezing cold!

I stared at the words. Maybe I wasn't going crazy. Maybe I had really called up a spirit.

I looked around one more time and then I wrote, "Hi. My name is Janice."

The pencil jumped out of my hand and wrote, "Hello, Janice." Once more it flopped over and lay still.

"Okay," I said to myself, "crazy or not, I get the idea."

I took the pencil and wrote, "Are you a ghost?"

The pencil jumped out of my hand again. It wrote, "We on the other side prefer to be called spirits."

I nodded and wrote, "What are you doing here?"

"Why shouldn't I be here?" the pencil wrote. "I was in the fifth grade just before I passed on."

"Oh, of course," I answered. "That makes sense."

"What are you doing right now?" asked Flora.

"I have to take a test in American history," I answered. "I hate it."

"Why?" asked Flora.

"It's boring," I wrote back.

"I will help you," answered Flora.

Just then, Ms. Hanover started to hand out the test papers. I grabbed the pencil tightly. I didn't want Flora to write anything while Ms. Hanover was around.

I bent over my test and chewed on my knuckles. I was afraid to start. But I was also afraid not to. I held on to the pencil so Ms. Hanover wouldn't notice anything weird. But it was really Flora who wrote down the answer to the first question. And the next. And the next . . .

I finished the test in no time at all. I hoped to hear something else from Flora. But she seemed to have gone away. I felt a little sad.

The next day I got my test back. There was a big *A* on the top of my paper. I was as happy as a clam. What a way to get good grades!

Later Flora contacted me again. "Boy, you sure knew all the answers," I wrote. "Thanks a lot."

"You're welcome," Flora wrote back. "Now maybe you can do me a favor."

"Sure. I guess I owe you one," I wrote. "What is it?"

"Just be my friend."

"We're friends already."

"Good," wrote Flora. "Then let me enter your body so we can talk without writing."

"You can do that?" I wrote back.

"Sure!"

"Why not?" I wrote. "It sounds like fun."

Suddenly an icy wind cut right through my body. In my mind I heard a voice say, "Thanks for inviting me in."

For the next few days, I talked with Flora in my head. It was weird but fun. I would just think something and Flora would answer me.

But then it stopped being fun. Flora began to take over. She made me do things *she* liked to do. She made me eat *her* favorite foods, which I hated. She made me watch TV shows that were stupid. And she made me talk to a boy named Jeremy Slats—the biggest nerd in my class! I was starting to feel like a stranger in my own body.

One day I had had enough. "Uh . . . Flora," I said in my head. "It's been real nice having you as a guest. But I would like to have my body all to myself again."

39

There was a long silence. Then Flora answered, "I like it here. I don't want to leave. Why don't *you* leave?"

My legs trembled. "But it's *my* body!" I shouted inside. "I'm not the one who's dead."

There was another long silence. I could tell Flora was thinking.

Then she answered, "That's true, isn't it?"

After school I was on my way to the library. I was waiting to cross the street when my mind suddenly went blank. The next thing I knew, I was in the middle of the street. A truck was coming right at me. I heard a lady scream, "Get out of the way!"

At the last minute, I jumped back. The truck went roaring by with a blast of its horn.

"Are you trying to get killed?" the lady said after she grabbed my arm.

I could only shake my head dumbly. "No, I wasn't trying to get killed," I told myself. Then suddenly I realized the truth. *Flora* was trying to get me killed.

Although I was shaking all over, I somehow made it to the library. I got my library book and sat at a table in the corner. I opened the book and my notebook, too. Suddenly I heard Flora's voice in my head.

"I'm bored. I want to go get a soda."

"No!" I said in a loud whisper. "This is my body, and I want to read my book."

Just then, the book flew up in the air and hit me in the nose.

"Ouch!" I cried.

Several people, including the librarian, looked over at me. I lowered my head and covered my face with my book. I was miserable. Maybe I should just give up and let Flora have my body, I thought.

Suddenly I saw my pencil move. It floated over my notebook and wrote:

"Flora Simmons! You come out of that body and return to class!"

I heard Flora cry inside me, "Oh, my gosh! It's Miss Primrose! She's found me!"

"You are a naughty girl. You have no right to

41

be in that child's body," the pencil continued writing. "If you don't come back to class right now, you will be left back again."

"You go to class on the *other side*?" I said in my head.

"Yes," Flora finally answered. "And Miss Primrose is the toughest teacher up there. That's one reason I wanted to stay in your body.

"Uh, look," she continued. "I'm really sorry about almost getting you killed. From my end it doesn't seem so bad, being dead myself. But I guess you have a lot of things you want to do yet."

"Right," I answered. "And I want to do them until I'm a hundred and one."

"That's asking *too* much," answered Flora.

"Okay, I'll settle for ninety-nine," I said.

Then the pencil wrote, "Flora, come back this minute. You're holding up the class."

"Oh, okay," I could feel Flora say in my mind.

And just when she was about to leave she said, "I really *am* sorry about everything. Do you think we can still be friends?"

I decided Flora probably wasn't such a bad

ghost after all. I shrugged. I was never one to hold a grudge.

"If you promise to behave from now on, you might have a ghost of a chance," I said with half a smile.

I could hear Flora say, "I will. And when you become a famous writer, if you ever need a ghost writer, I'll be there."

I had to laugh out loud. One thing I've always liked in a person, ghost or no ghost, is a sense of humor.

Tommy's Birthday Present

KEVIN RODE HIS bike along the path through the park. The cold January wind made his face and hands sting. He wished he hadn't forgotten his gloves. He hunched into his navy parka and pumped hard to keep himself warm.

The large park near the center of town was Kevin's shortcut home. But now Kevin wondered if he should have come this way. The park was so much colder without any buildings to block the wind. Besides, it was already getting dark, and there was no one else around.

He was about to turn back. But then he came to a large frozen pond. He knew the pond was halfway through the park. So he decided to keep on going.

The wind moaned through the trees. It

sounded like a howling dog. Or—he thought with a shudder—like a howling *ghost.*

Suddenly Kevin felt as if someone were watching him. He turned his head around.

His bike almost went off the path. Kevin turned forward again quickly and took control. But now he couldn't believe his own eyes. Just ahead of him on a bench sat a boy.

Where had he come from? Kevin was sure no one had been there a second ago. A shiver went up his spine.

Kevin stopped his bike in front of the boy. He was about Kevin's own age. He had straight brown hair and a ghostly white face. The boy raised his eyes toward Kevin. His large black pupils stared straight ahead without expression. But the whites were all red, as if the boy had been crying.

There was something about the boy that sent goose bumps up Kevin's arms. He felt like pedaling away as quickly as he could. But the boy seemed so sad and lonely. Kevin couldn't leave without talking to him. So he gave the boy a friendly smile and said, "Hi."

"H-hello," the boy replied. He wiped one eye with the back of his hand.

"Is something the matter?" Kevin asked as he got off his bike. "I mean, are you lost or something?"

The boy didn't answer Kevin's question. Instead he just stared and said, "My name's Tommy—Tommy Cavendish."

"My name's Kevin Reynolds. I'm new around here. My family moved into town two weeks ago.

"Do you go to McKinley, too?" Kevin continued. "I've never seen you around school."

Again the boy ignored his question. As if he were talking to himself, he said, "Tomorrow is my birthday. I'll be eleven."

This kid is strange, Kevin thought. His voice is strange, too. It sounds like it's coming from the other end of a long tunnel.

"No kidding," Kevin said finally. "I'm eleven myself."

The boy's lower lip trembled.

"But I won't be getting any presents," he said. "My mom and dad gave them away."

"Gave them away?" Kevin repeated. He didn't know what else to say.

"They could have put them with me," Tommy went on. "I would have known."

"Oh, yeah, sure," said Kevin with a fake smile. "Well, I—ah, better be going now." And he started to get back on his bike.

Suddenly Tommy's eyes widened. He sat up straight and blurted out, "I was going to get a bunch of Robot Riders toys. I love Robot Riders."

Kevin stopped and smiled, this time for real. "I do too," he replied. "How about that new Space Car? I just got it for Christmas. Isn't it great?"

"I don't know that one," said Tommy. "But I sure like the new Assault Copter."

Kevin was puzzled. The Assault Copter was at least three years old. It had been one of *his* birthday presents when he was *eight.*

"Uh—well, I wouldn't call the Assault Copter new," Kevin finally answered. "It's been out a long time. I used to play with it when I was younger. And I tell you, I really destroyed it. But

I wouldn't let my mom throw it out. I still have it somewhere in my closet."

Tommy nodded in understanding. "Robot Riders are terrific," he said.

Kevin agreed, and for the next ten minutes they talked about Robot Riders. Kevin forgot about the cold. He decided that Tommy wasn't as weird as he had first thought. In fact, Kevin was starting to like him a lot.

All at once Kevin remembered the time and he shot a look at his watch.

"Wow! I've got to get home," he said.

Then he paused a moment.

"Say, I don't want to be pushy. But if you're having a party tomorrow, could I come?"

Tommy looked as if he would cry again. "I'm not having a party, and I'm not getting any presents."

Kevin felt a sinking feeling in his stomach. He wished now that he hadn't said anything.

"Well," Kevin finally said. "Can I come and visit you tomorrow anyway? We can talk about Robot Riders some more."

"Visit me?" Tommy answered. A faraway look crept into his eyes. "I guess you can. That is, if you're sure you want to."

"I want to," Kevin said. "Why don't you give me your address."

"I'm at the very end of Fairlawn Road," Tommy said,

"Great. That's easy to remember."

Kevin got on his bike and looked down at Tommy. "Aren't *you* going home?" he asked.

Tommy looked up at him, his face paler than ever. "I'll be okay here. I have to go back soon."

Kevin nodded. Tommy sure had a funny way of putting things.

"Well, see you tomorrow then," Kevin said, smiling. Then, with a final look back at Tommy, he pumped his bike hard and rode off. The air seemed even colder than before.

During supper Kevin thought about Tommy. What could be wrong with his parents? Why weren't they giving him a birthday party? And why had they given away his presents? Kevin felt more and more sorry for him.

Before bed, Kevin pulled his Space Car down from its shelf. As he looked at it, he got a great idea. The car was still like new. He could wrap it up and surprise Tommy with it for his birthday.

The next day was just as cold and gloomy as the day before had been. But with the Space Car wrapped in bright paper and with a birthday card to go with it, Kevin felt warm and cheerful.

Right after school, Kevin got on his bike and headed for Fairlawn Road.

The road twisted a lot, and the houses became farther apart. After he passed a small white house, the road curved behind a low hill. Fifty yards later, Fairlawn Road ended. But there was no house in sight—only a small cemetery!

Kevin felt a chill go through him that had nothing to do with the weather.

What was going on?

Then he realized that Tommy must have meant the house he had just passed.

Kevin rode back, went up to the door, and rang the bell. He heard footsteps inside. Then the door opened. A thin, cheerful-looking woman about seventy years old smiled at him.

"What can I do for you, young man?" she asked.

"Does Tommy Cavendish live here?" Kevin asked.

The woman gave him a funny look. Then she said, "Come in. It's too cold to stand out here talking."

Once Kevin was inside, the woman had him sit down on a bright yellow chair.

"Now, tell me," she said. "Why are you asking about Tommy Cavendish?"

Kevin told her about their meeting in the park. At that, the woman bit her lip. She looked shocked.

"Don't you know about Tommy Cavendish?" she asked.

"What do you mean?" asked Kevin.

"Why, the poor boy drowned in the pond in that park near the center of town. Fell right through the ice, poor boy."

She looked at Kevin and shook her head sadly.

"It was about three years ago, the day before

his eleventh birthday," the woman continued. "His poor parents were so heartbroken, they gave all his presents to a children's home."

Although Kevin was still sitting, he suddenly felt dizzy. He held on to the arm of the chair to steady himself.

"B-but if he's dead, how could I have seen him in the park?"

The woman clasped her hands in front of her and looked away. Then she faced Kevin again and said, "I don't know the answer to that."

Kevin nodded sadly and got ready to leave. But a sudden thought occurred to him.

"Could you tell me where his grave is?" he asked.

"Why, of course," the woman replied. "It's just beyond the cemetery gate."

Kevin gasped. "So that's what Tommy meant when he said he was at the end of Fairlawn Road," he told himself.

Kevin thanked the woman and headed back to the cemetery. He went through the open gate and almost immediately saw the tombstone.

THOMAS CAVENDISH
1977–1988
May his soul
rest in peace

Kevin felt a lump in his throat as he stood over the grave. He looked at the present he was holding in his hand. Then he placed it gently on top of the stone.

A sudden warm breeze blew softly against his face. Kevin wondered if it was Tommy. He felt that somehow it must be.

"Happy birthday, Tommy," he said as he got on his bike and slowly pedaled away. "I hope you like your present."